My Fairytale Time

PUSS in BOOTS

Miles Kelly

There was once a miller who had three sons. When he died, he left the mill to his eldest son and a donkey to his middle son.

The youngest son was given the miller's cat. "What am I to do with a cat?" he said. Imagine his surprise when Puss replied, "Give me some boots and a bag and you shall see!"

So the youngest son gave Puss some boots and
a bag. Puss went to a field and put carrots in the
bag, then he hid in the grass. Before long, a rabbit
hopped into the bag, tempted by the carrots.

Off Puss ran to the palace, where he offered the rabbit to the king as a gift from the Marquis of Carabas. The king was delighted.

Help!

The next day, Puss said to the miller's son, "Come to the river and help me fish." Puss knew the king would be driving by in his carriage.

"Quick, get into the water!" said Puss. The miller's son did, just as the carriage passed by. Then Puss hid his master's clothes.

"STOP!" cried Puss, and he ran in front of the carriage. "My master, the Marquis of Carabas, has been robbed! Thieves stole his clothes as he swam in the river!"

The king ordered fine clothes to be brought for the miller's son. Then he was invited to ride in the carriage with the king and the princess.

In the meantime, Puss ran ahead of the carriage. He met some workers gathering hay in the fields.

"When the king's carriage drives by, the king will ask who owns this land," said Puss. "Say it belongs to the Marquis of Carabas." Sure enough, this is what happened. The king was impressed.

Bang Bang!

Once again, Puss ran ahead. He came to a big castle where he knew an ogre lived. Puss knocked loudly at the gate and a servant let him in.

Puss was taken to meet the ogre, and he bowed down low. "What do you want?" the ogre growled.

GRRR!

Puss was scared, but he said, "I've heard you can do amazing magic Mr Ogre, and turn yourself into any animal. But can you turn into a lion?" The ogre immediately became a roaring lion.

ROAARR!

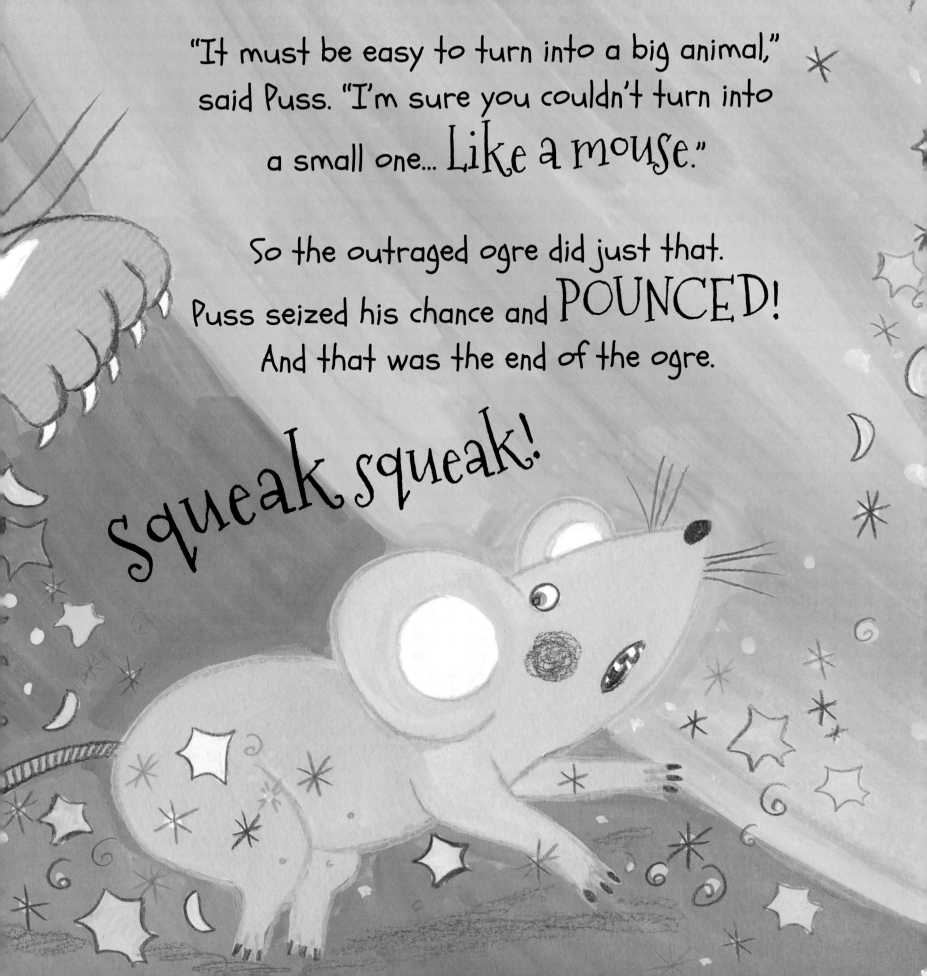

"It must be easy to turn into a big animal," said Puss. "I'm sure you couldn't turn into a small one... Like a mouse."

So the outraged ogre did just that.
Puss seized his chance and POUNCED!
And that was the end of the ogre.

Squeak squeak!

The servants in the castle were very happy. They had been under the ogre's spell. Pleased to be free, they agreed to become servants of the
Marquis of Carabas.

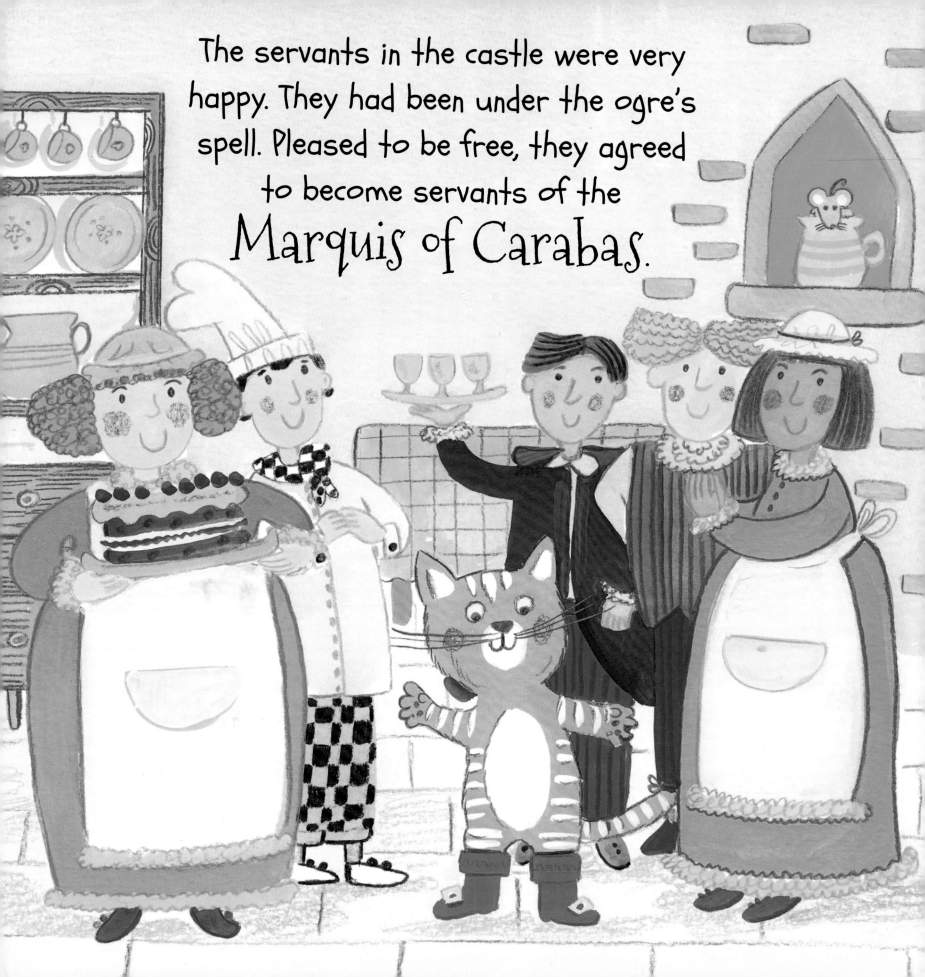

Suddenly, Puss heard the King's carriage approach.

"Prepare a feast for the king and the Marquis of Carabas!" he said.

Welcome!

The carriage stopped and the king stepped out, amazed. "Welcome to the castle of the Marquis of Carabas!" said Puss, bowing low.

They all sat down to a huge feast. The miller's son and the princess had fallen in love. The king offered the Marquis of Carabas his daughter's hand in marriage.

The next day the princess and the miller's son were married. Puss was very pleased at the way his plan had worked out.

Congratulations!

Puss spent the rest of his days living in luxury – and the only time he ever chased mice was for his own amusement.

Eeek!